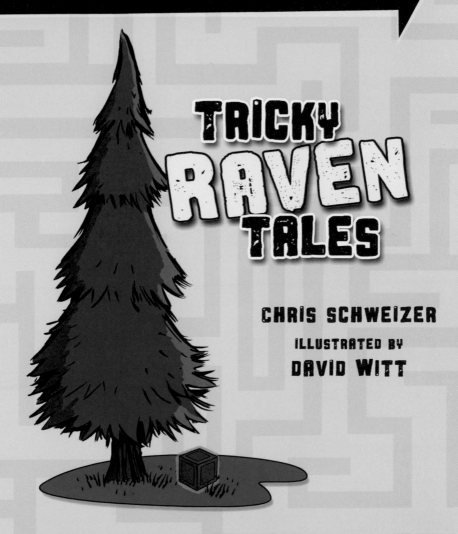

TRICKY JOURNEYS #4

TRICKY RAVEN TALES

CHRIS SCHWEIZER

ILLUSTRATED BY

DAVID WITT

GRAPHIC UNIVERSE™ • MINNEAPOLIS • NEW YORK

Story by Chris Schweizer

Illustrations by David Witt

Coloring by John Novak

Lettering by Grace Lu

Copyright © 2011 by Lerner Publishing Group, Inc.

Graphic Universe™ and Tricky Journeys™ are trademarks of Lerner Publishing Group, Inc.

Graphic Universe™
A division of Lerner Publishing Group, Inc.
241 First Avenue North
Minneapolis, MN 55401 U.S.A.

Website address: www.lernerbooks.com

Main body text set in CC Dave Gibbons Lower 14/22.
Typeface provided by Comicraft/Active Images.

Library of Congress Cataloging-in-Publication Data

Schweizer, Chris.
       Tricky raven tales / by Chris Schweizer ; illustrated by David Witt.
          p.   cm. — (Tricky journeys)
       Summary: Raven, who loves to play tricks, seeks food and shelter after a storm destroys her nest, and the reader helps her make choices as she encounters many other creatures, some friendly and some dangerous.
       ISBN 978–0–7613–6603–4 (lib. bdg. : alk. paper) 1. Plot-your-own stories. 2. Graphic novels. [1. Graphic novels. 2. Raven (Legendary character)—Fiction. 3. Tricksters— Fiction. 4. Animals—Fiction. 5. Plot-your-own stories.] I. Witt, David, ill. II. Title.
       PZ7.7.S39Rav 2011
       741.5'973—dc22   2010045682

Manufactured in the United States of America
1 – CG – 7/15/11

Are you ready
for your Tricky Journeys™?
You'll find yourself right smack in
the middle of this story's tricks,
jokes, thrills, and fun.

Each page tells what happens to Raven
and her friends. YOU get to decide what
happens next. Read each page until you
reach a choice. Then pick the
choice YOU like best.

But be careful...one wrong choice
could land Raven in a mess that
even she can't trick
her way out of.

"That was some storm," Raven says. She's sitting in a pile of broken twigs. The wind has blown her nest from the trees. She wipes wet leaves off her face. "My blanket blew away in the wind! If I don't get warm soon, I'll freeze!"

Raven looks up and down to see if her blanket is stuck in a nearby tree. Soon she notices an orange glow from deep in the woods. "Maybe someone has a fire going!" she says, rising from the ground. "That will warm me up!"

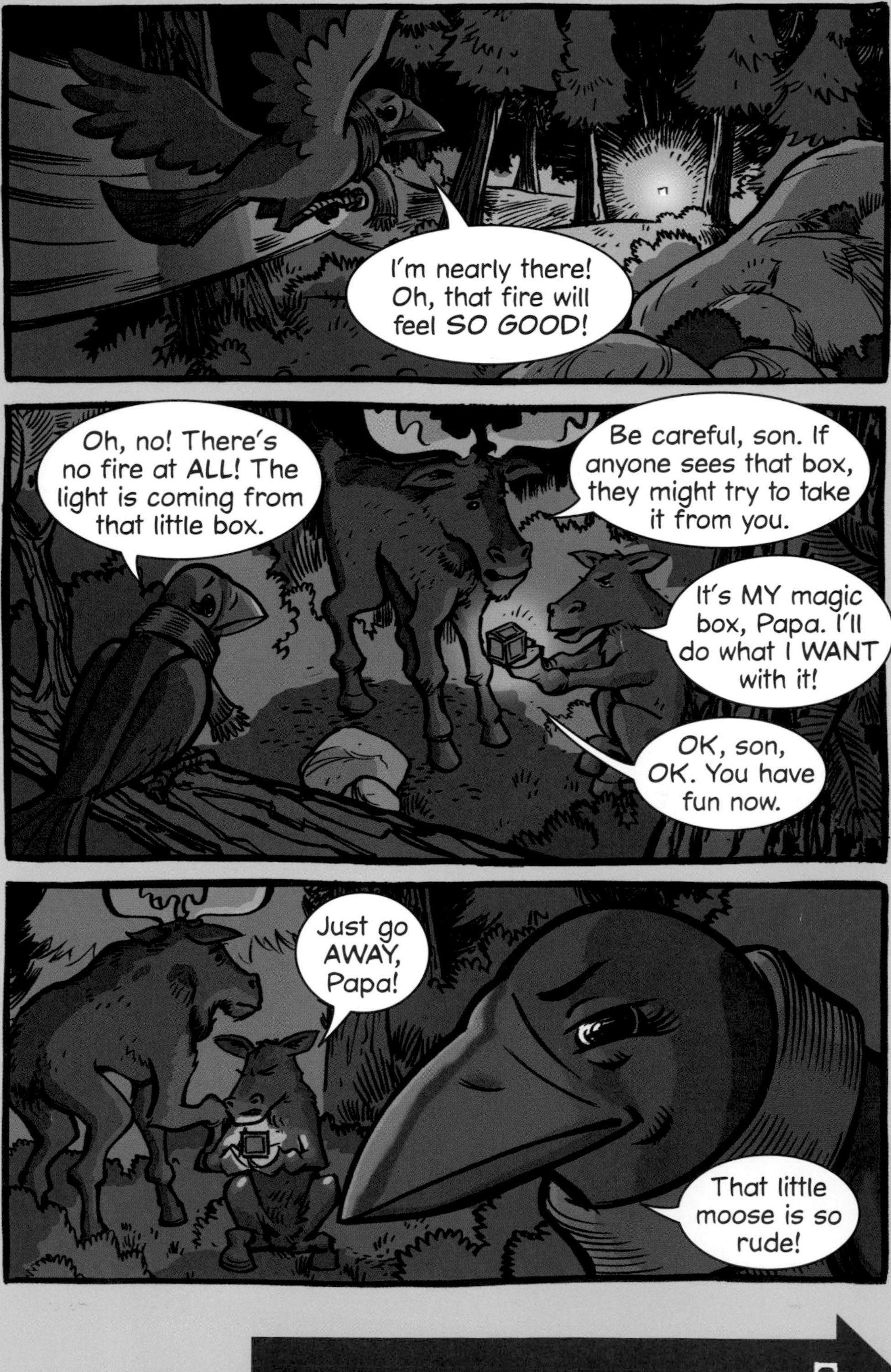
I'm nearly there! Oh, that fire will feel SO GOOD!
Oh, no! There's no fire at ALL! The light is coming from that little box.
Be careful, son. If anyone sees that box, they might try to take it from you.
It's MY magic box, Papa. I'll do what I WANT with it!
OK, son, OK. You have fun now.
Just go AWAY, Papa!
That little moose is so rude!

"I never talk to my parents like that," thinks Raven. "I should teach him a lesson."

If Raven gives the young moose a good scare,

TURN TO PAGE **46.**

If Raven tries to take the moose's box,

TURN TO PAGE **30.**

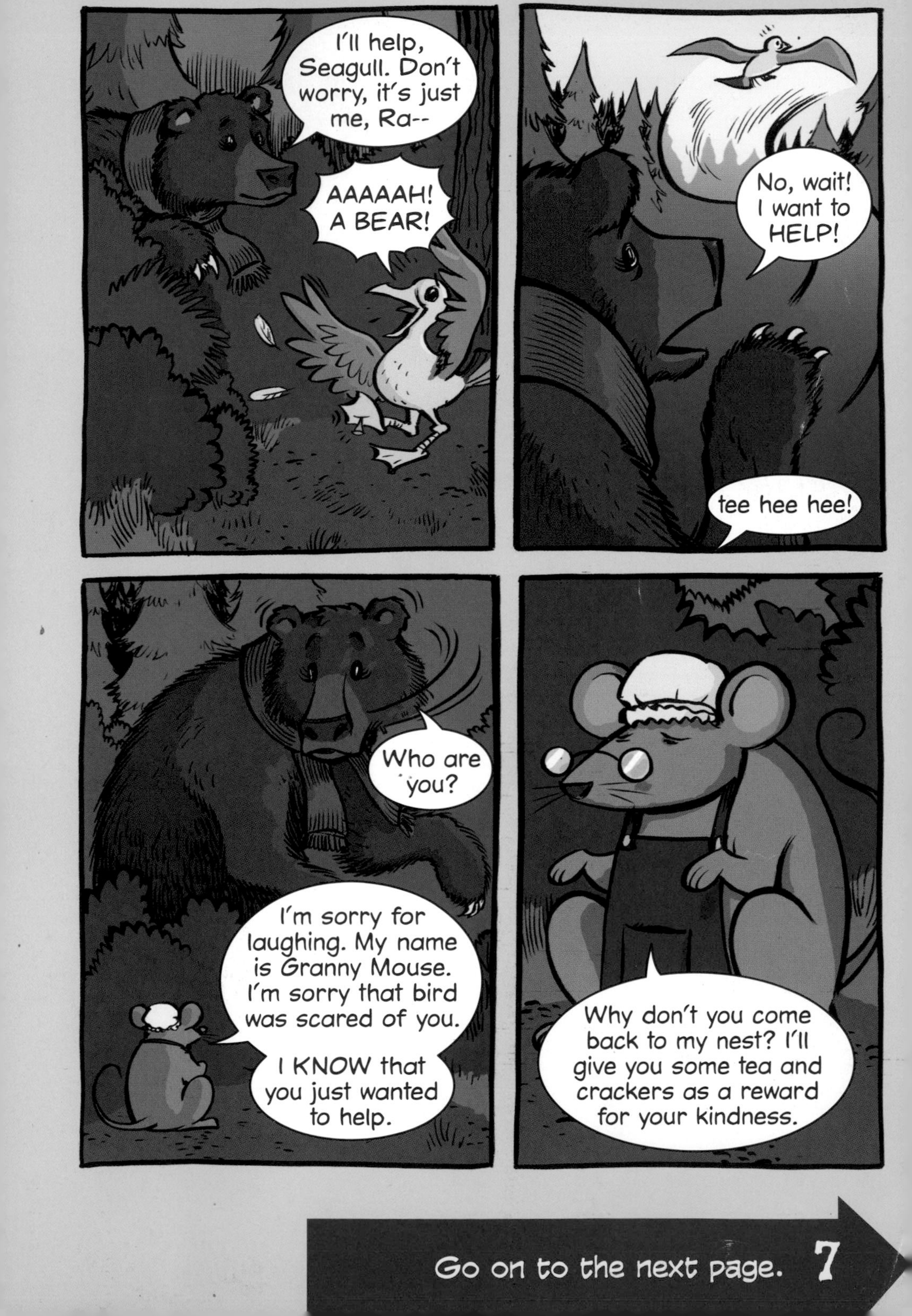
I'll help, Seagull. Don't worry, it's just me, Ra--
AAAAAH! A BEAR!
No, wait! I want to HELP!
tee hee hee!
Who are you?
I'm sorry for laughing. My name is Granny Mouse. I'm sorry that bird was scared of you.
I KNOW that you just wanted to help.
Why don't you come back to my nest? I'll give you some tea and crackers as a reward for your kindness.

"That sounds great!" says Raven, licking her big bear lips. As she follows Granny Mouse deeper into the forest, Raven finds it hard to move through the tight trees. "Maybe I should change back into a bird," she thinks, "but I don't want to scare this nice old lady."

If Raven changes back into her regular body,

TURN TO PAGE 55.

If Raven stays in her bear body,

TURN TO PAGE 24.

8

Raven looks at her magic box and thinks hard. Suddenly, she looks just like Mr. Pelican!

She opens the Pelicans' door. "I thought I'd catch more fish to sell," says Raven.

Mrs. Pelican looks at Raven suspiciously. "How will you carry more fish?" she asks.

"I'll use a cart, of course." says Raven. "Your head must be foggy. Can you even remember how we learned to fish from your beak?"

"I remember fine!" says Mrs. Pelican. "You caught an old trout. He promised you a wish if you let him go. You wished for a way to fish at home. Now you can pour water in my mouth and reach through it into the ocean."

She fills her beak with water again.

Raven realizes that she doesn't have a fishing pole—the REAL Mr. Pelican took it with him!

If Raven looks around for an extra fishing pole,

TURN TO PAGE 62.

If Raven tries to catch the fish with her bare hands,

TURN TO PAGE 27.

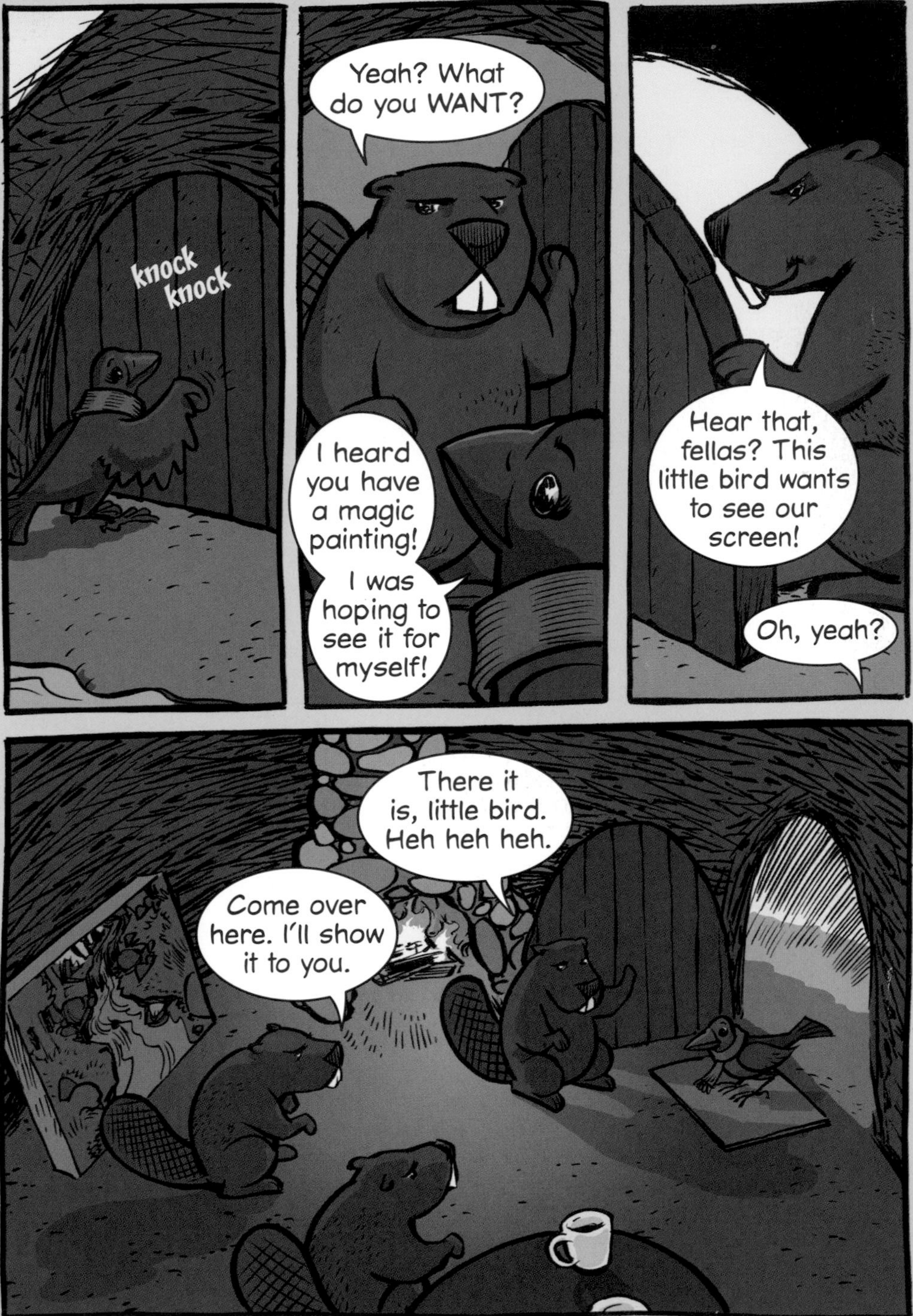
knock knock
Yeah? What do you WANT?
I heard you have a magic painting!
I was hoping to see it for myself!
Hear that, fellas? This little bird wants to see our screen!
Oh, yeah?
There it is, little bird. Heh heh heh.
Come over here. I'll show it to you.

"These beavers are up to no good," thinks Raven. "I want to see that picture, but I don't want to get into any trouble. Maybe I should grab it and fly off. Or maybe I can trick them into leaving me alone with it."

If Raven tries to fly away with the painting,

TURN TO PAGE
33.

If Raven tries to get the beavers to leave her alone with the painting,

TURN TO PAGE
51.

"Fine," says Raven. "I'll leave. But I'm taking THIS with me!" She grabs Crow's blanket and jumps out of the nest.

She doesn't get very far. The blanket goes tight and slips out of Raven's claws. She loses her balance and tumbles to the ground!

Crow looks down at his dazed cousin. "I keep my blanket tied to one side of the nest," he says. "That way I can make it into a roof when it rains. Now SCRAM!"

Raven sulks off into the woods. She still needs a way to get warm. But as far as help from her cousin goes, this is

THE END

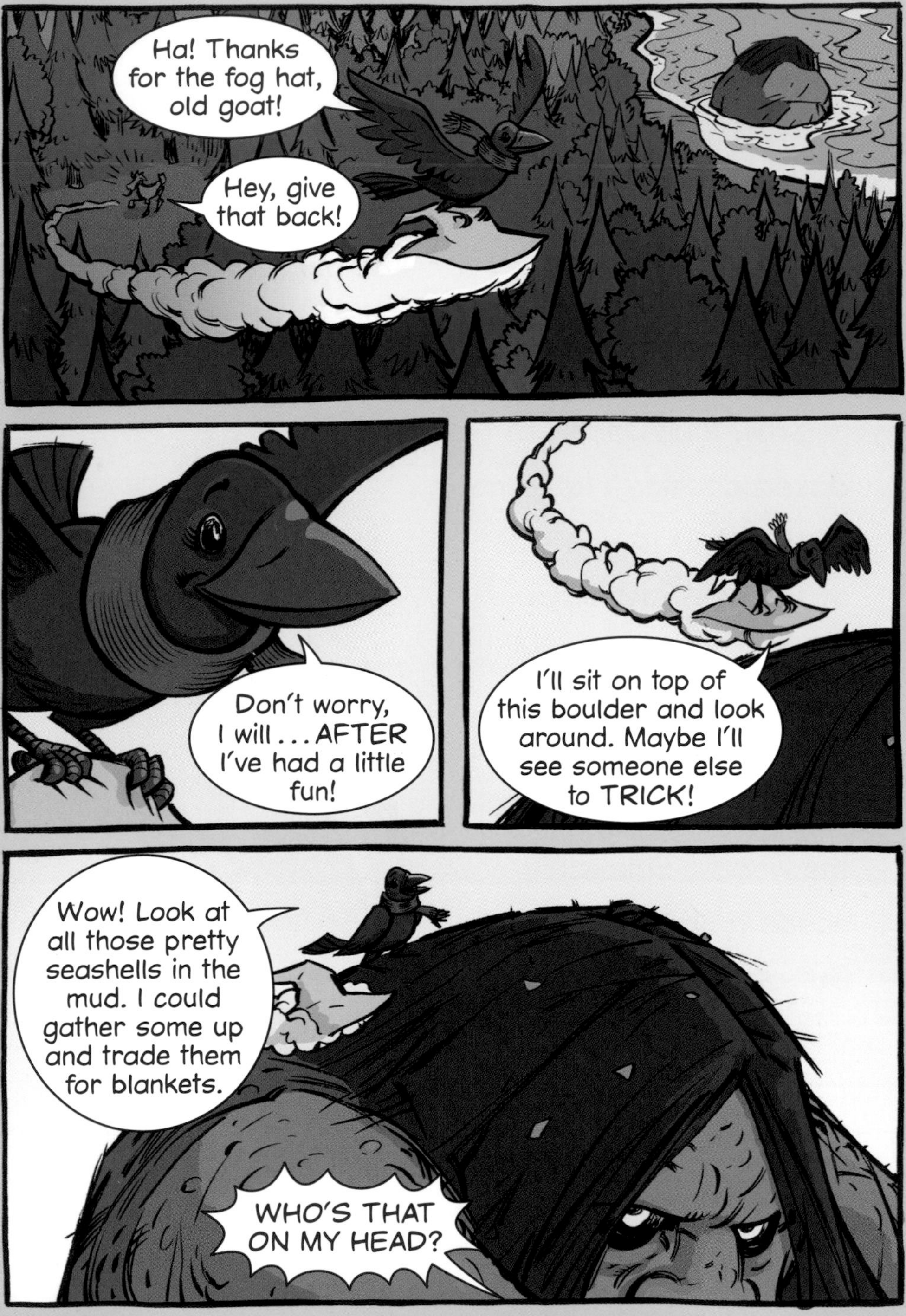
Ha! Thanks for the fog hat, old goat!
Hey, give that back!
Don't worry, I will . . . AFTER I've had a little fun!
I'll sit on top of this boulder and look around. Maybe I'll see someone else to TRICK!
Wow! Look at all those pretty seashells in the mud. I could gather some up and trade them for blankets.
WHO'S THAT ON MY HEAD?

Raven jumps, surprised by the booming voice. She's not on a boulder at all. She's on top of a giant!

"Pardon me!" says Raven, flapping her wings. "I thought you were a big rock!"

The giant turns her head with a CREAK. Dust falls off her. "What a rude thing to say to a nice old lady!" growls the giant. "I should give you a good slap!" With a groan, the giant stands up. Raven can see a wet patch of beach that used to be underwater.

"My goodness!" thinks Raven. "This old giant is so big that the water rises when she sits in it!"

The giant swings a huge hand at Raven. Raven ducks. "That was close!" she thinks. "If this giant doesn't calm down, I might end up flattened!" The giant swings at Raven a second time. "I should get out of here," Raven thinks. "But those shells looked so nice. I'll never get a chance like this again!"

If Raven tries to calm the giant down,

TURN TO PAGE 34.

If Raven tries to gather shells,

TURN TO PAGE 61.

16

"I don't need to hear you sing!" says Raven in a booming walrus voice. "Everyone says you're wonderful. I want to sign you up on the SPOT!"

"Well, I AM a truly great singer!" says Crow. "When do I start? Next spring?"

Raven shakes her big walrus head. "You start today, my boy! Fly out! The royal iceberg is just a little ways out to sea. Everyone else will be there soon." Raven watches Crow fly away, singing his scratchy songs.

She changes back into a bird. Then she flies up into Crow's warm nest and wraps herself in his blanket. "Much better!" Raven says and drifts off to sleep.

THE END

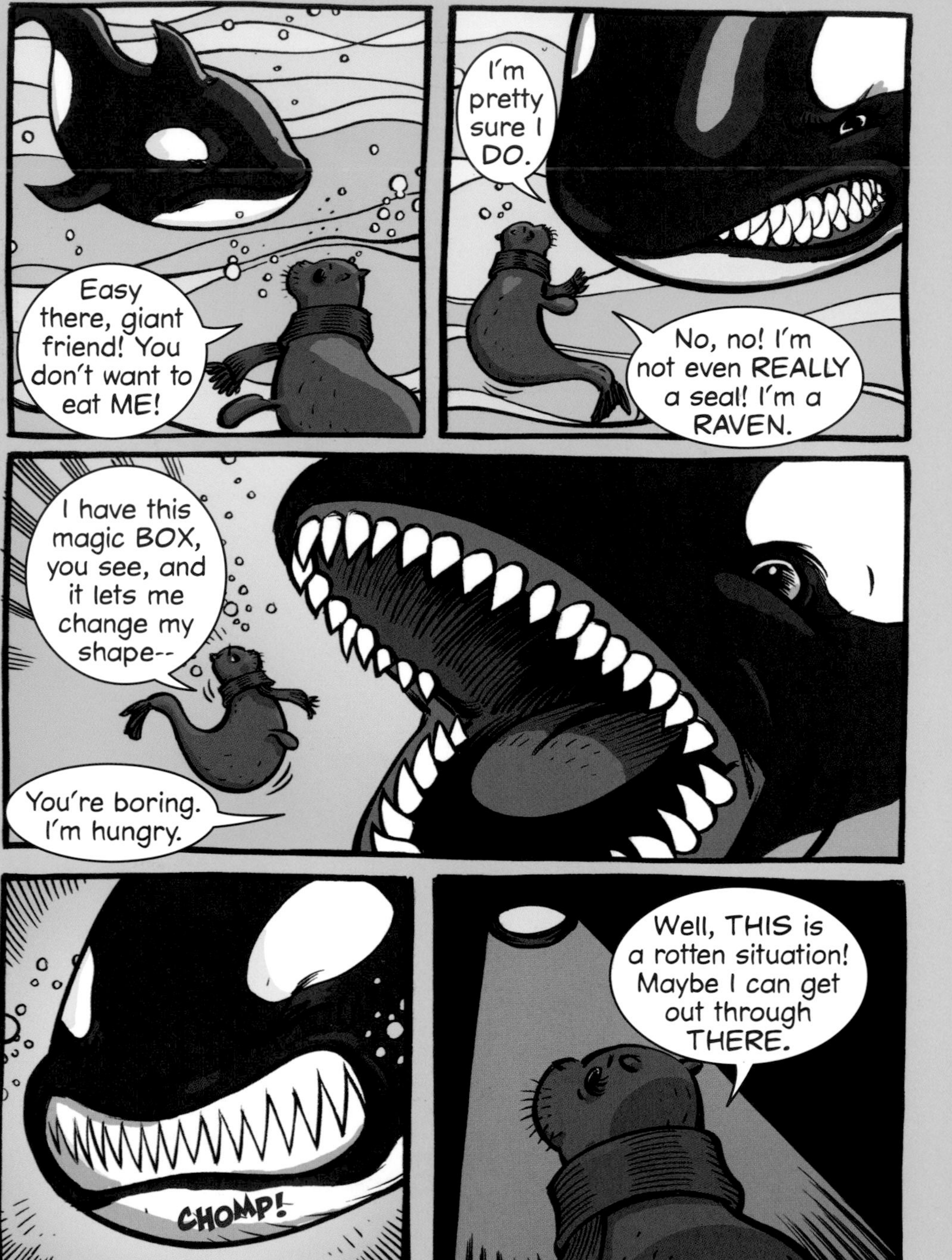
Easy there, giant friend! You don't want to eat ME!
I'm pretty sure I DO.
No, no! I'm not even REALLY a seal! I'm a RAVEN.
I have this magic BOX, you see, and it lets me change my shape--
You're boring. I'm hungry.
CHOMP!
Well, THIS is a rotten situation! Maybe I can get out through THERE.

 Go on to the next page.

Raven uses the magic box to change back into her old self. "Maybe now I can fit through that hole," she says. She flaps her wings and flies toward it.

She wiggles her head through the hole. At first she's underwater. But by the time she gets halfway out, the whale has surfaced.

"Stop!" yells the whale. "You're stretching out my blowhole!"

"Next time, don't eat someone as clever as I am!" replies Raven. She wriggles free and flies up into the sky.

Raven can't wait to get back to land and cuddle up in a blanket. This adventure has been too scary for her taste. She's glad that it has reached

THE END

"Mr. Goat!" calls Raven. The old goat turns around. "I think that's a wonderful hat!"

The goat snorts. "This hat is nothing but trouble!" he says. "Can't you see the fog pouring out?"

"That's what makes it so wonderful!" Raven laughs. "My cousin Crow lives nearby. Would you help me play a trick on him?"

"I know Crow!" exclaims the goat. "He ate all of my cabbages last year. Let's do it!"

The old goat follows Raven into the woods. They hear a scratchy song coming from a nest high in the trees.

"Sounds like he's up there, singing with that horrible voice," says the old goat. "Should we trick him in his nest or try to get him to leave it?"

If Raven says that they should trick him in his nest,

TURN TO PAGE 40.

If Raven decides they should try to get him out of the nest,

TURN TO PAGE 25.

21

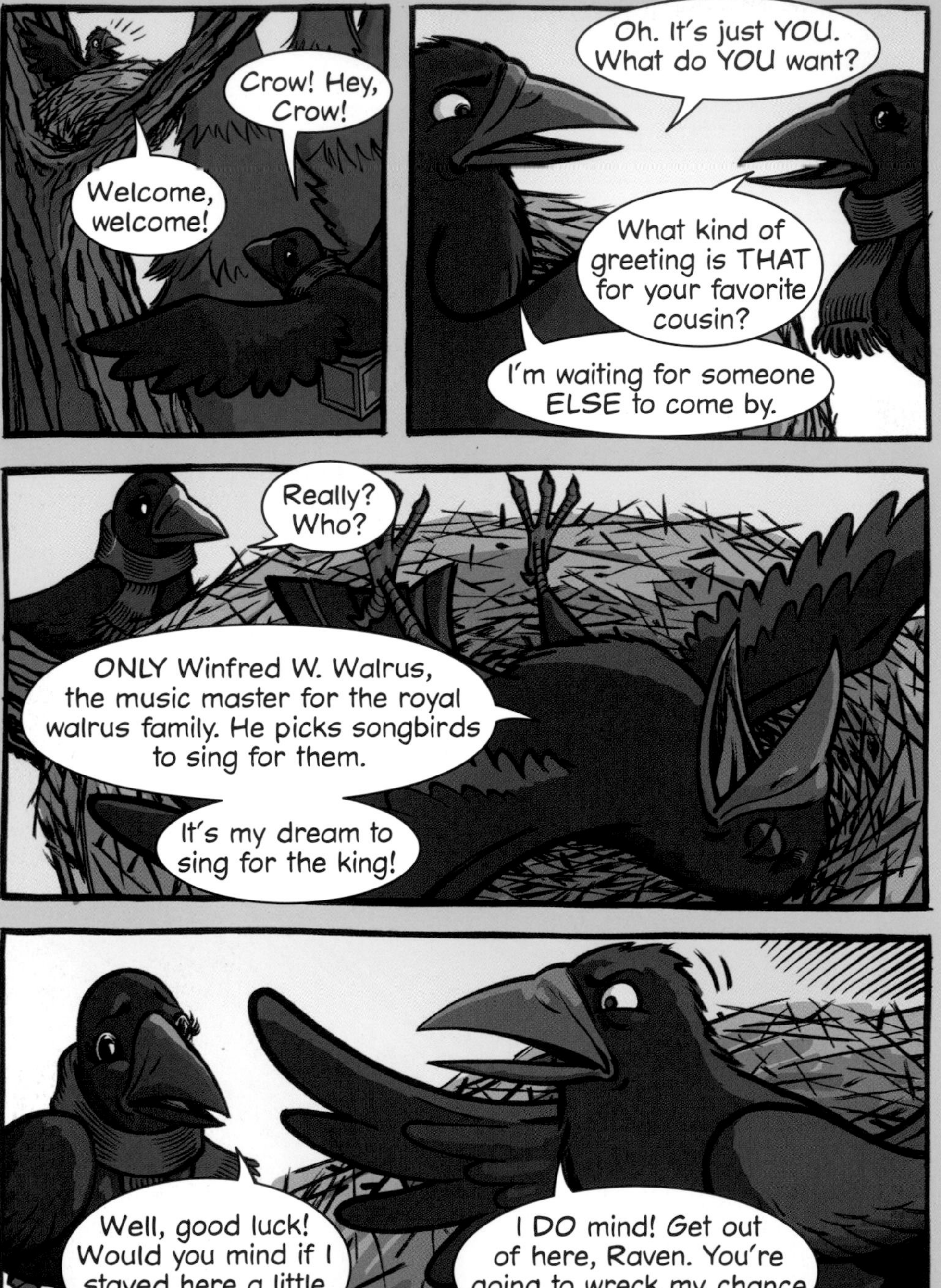
Welcome, welcome!
Crow! Hey, Crow!
Oh. It's just YOU. What do YOU want?
What kind of greeting is THAT for your favorite cousin?
I'm waiting for someone ELSE to come by.
Really? Who?
ONLY Winfred W. Walrus, the music master for the royal walrus family. He picks songbirds to sing for them.
It's my dream to sing for the king!
Well, good luck! Would you mind if I stayed here a little while to warm--
I DO mind! Get out of here, Raven. You're going to wreck my chance to be famous!

Go on to the next page.

Raven can't believe her cousin's rudeness! Crow has a blanket and a warm nest, but he refuses to share. "I'll get even," she thinks.

If Raven uses the magic box to trick Crow,

TURN TO PAGE 59.

If Raven takes Crow's blanket,

TURN TO PAGE 13.

Raven lumbers along on her big paws. She follows Granny Mouse between two large trees. Raven is halfway through when she feels a squeeze. She's stuck! She drops her box.

"Help!" says Raven. "I'm too big! If you hand me that box, I can turn back into a bird."

"You poor dear!" Granny Mouse squeaks. "Getting stuck must have made you loopy! I'll go gather more mice to push you free. It will take a lot of mice, though. I may be gone awhile." She scurries away.

Raven looks at the box, just out of reach, and cries big bear tears. It's going to be a long wait.

THE END

Let's get Crow to come HERE. Are you still mad about the cabbages he stole?

Mad? I'm FURIOUS!

What if we trick him into giving US all the food he has in his nest?

THAT will teach him!

Crow! Hey, Crow! Look what I got!

Raven, is that you? What do you--

AAAAH!!! What happened to YOU?!

I have a magic acorn! It lets me change my body however I want. I can grow LEGS for running fast or a LONG NECK for reaching high branches. I get lots of FOOD!

Go on to the next page.

Food is Crow's favorite thing. "I want that acorn!" Crow says. "Will you give it to me?"

"Then I won't be able to gather food so easily," Raven says.

"You can have some of the food I gather!" Crow says. The goat drops an acorn. Crow cackles with glee and picks it up.

"You have to fly to the mountain the first time you change!" Raven calls to him. "The mountain is far away," she whispers to goat. "We can run away with his food while he's gone!"

"What a dope!" says Crow as he flies off. "Tricked into such a bad deal. Now I'll get more food, and Raven will stay hungry!"

Silly Crow. He'll find out soon who really got tricked!

THE END

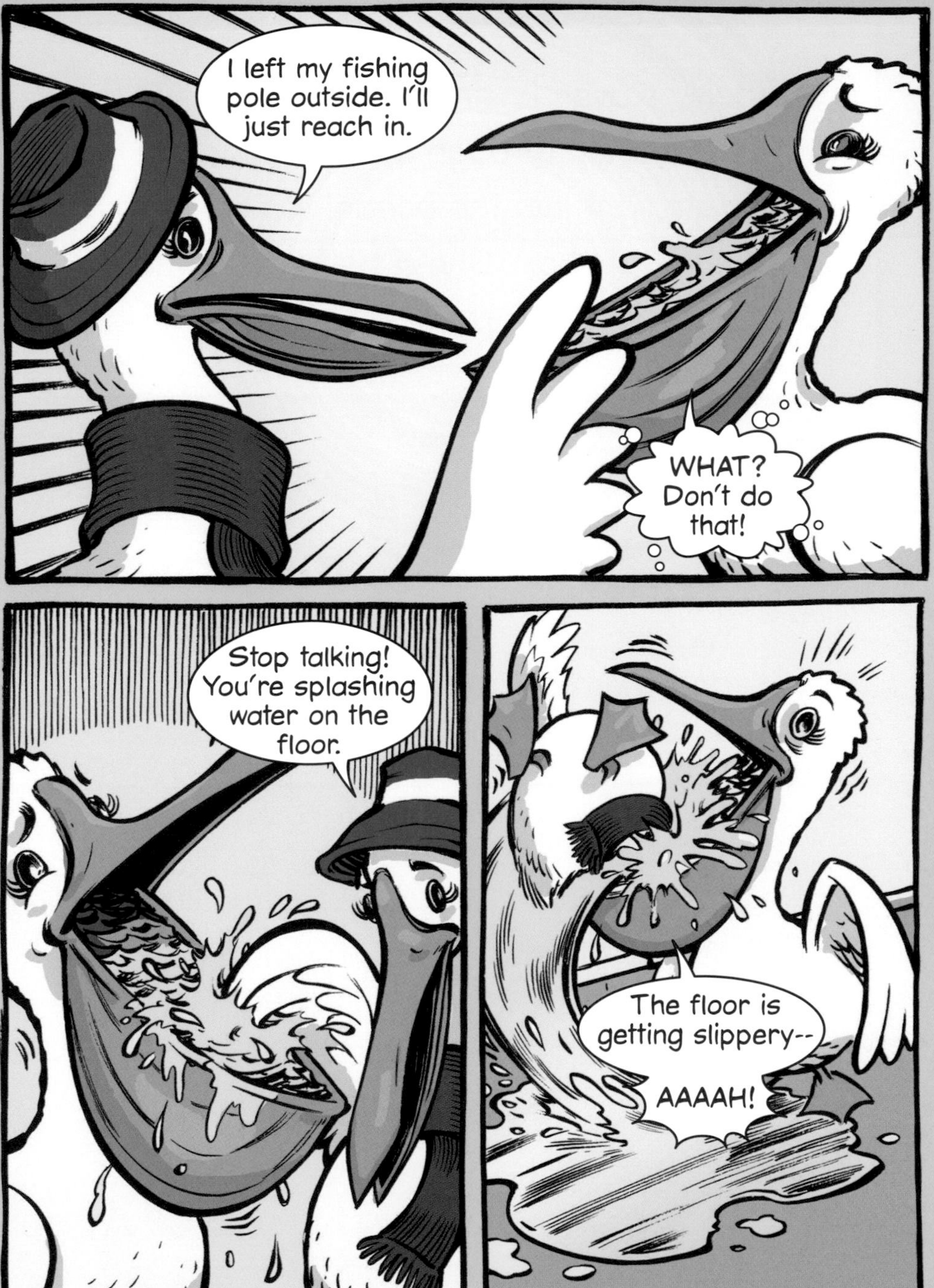
I left my fishing pole outside. I'll just reach in.
WHAT? Don't do that!
Stop talking! You're splashing water on the floor.
The floor is getting slippery--
AAAAH!

Go on to the next page.

Suddenly Raven is sinking deep into swirling waters. She fell through Mrs. Pelican's beak—straight into the ocean! Raven still has the magic box. She'd better use it to change quickly!

If Raven changes back to her regular body and swims to the surface,

TURN TO PAGE 56.

If Raven changes into a fish so that she can breathe underwater,

TURN TO PAGE 42.

Raven transforms back into a bird. She hops out of the woods. "I can help!" she says.

Seagull holds out his foot. Raven looks at it very closely. "I don't see a thorn," she says.

Without warning, Seagull pushes Raven over! Her magic box tumbles from out of her wings.

"I saw you use the box to change into a bear," says Seagull. "Seagulls have lots of practice standing on one leg. It was easy to push you over while you were looking at my foot. Now the box is mine!" He disappears into the sky.

Raven sits on the ground, sore and disappointed. Her warm evening has reached

THE END

"Psssst!" whispers Raven. The little moose looks up and sees her sitting on a branch.

"What do YOU want?" he asks.

Raven flutters down beside him. "Who does your father think he is?" she asks. "He can't tell you what to do with your own things."

"I know, right?" says the moose. "I'm getting so tired of it!"

"We should teach him a lesson!" says Raven. "I can help! Your father is worried about someone taking your box. But you're too tough to let anybody steal your stuff."

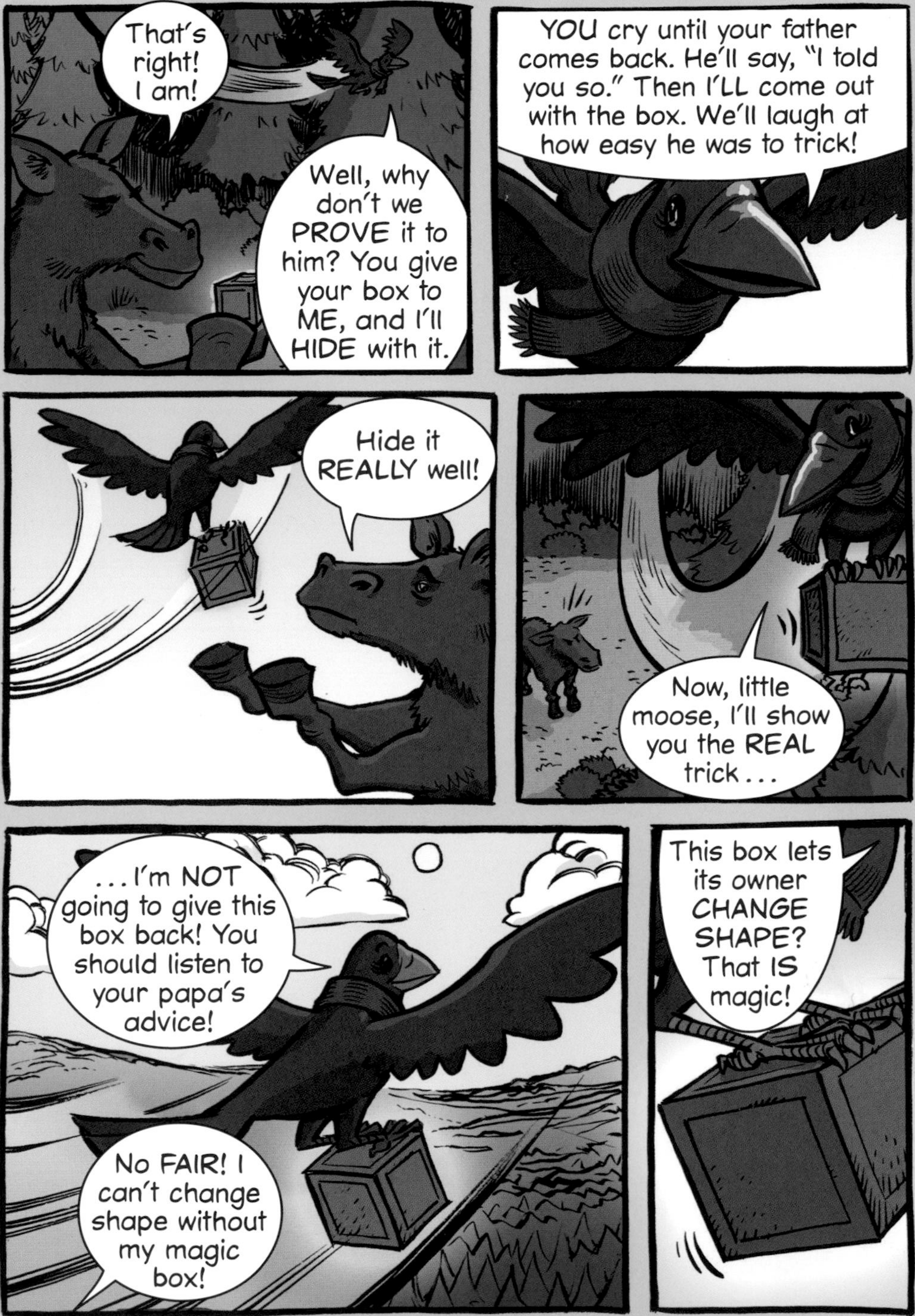
That's right! I am!
Well, why don't we PROVE it to him? You give your box to ME, and I'll HIDE with it.
YOU cry until your father comes back. He'll say, "I told you so." Then I'LL come out with the box. We'll laugh at how easy he was to trick!
Hide it REALLY well!
Now, little moose, I'll show you the REAL trick . . .
. . . I'm NOT going to give this box back! You should listen to your papa's advice!
No FAIR! I can't change shape without my magic box!
This box lets its owner CHANGE SHAPE? That IS magic!

Go on to the next page.

Raven sees smoke in the distance. "I bet my new box could help me get close to that fire," she thinks. "But if I had fur instead of feathers, I wouldn't NEED fire. I'd be warm! Maybe I should visit my cousin, Crow. He lives nearby. He might help me decide what to do."

If Raven heads for the smoke,

TURN TO PAGE
53.

If Raven turns into an animal with fur,

TURN TO PAGE
49.

If Raven goes to see her cousin Crow,

TURN TO PAGE
22.

Raven walks up to the big canvas. The river in the picture is moving! She can't believe her eyes. Quickly, she grabs the painting! The beavers try to grab her, but she darts to the side and bursts out the door.

Raven takes flight. She gasps as a fish drops out of the painting. Soon another fish falls out. "This doesn't just SHOW a river," thinks Raven. "There IS a river in here!"

Raven smiles. She still has to rebuild her nest, but at least she can work on a full stomach. All she needs to do is reach into the painting and pull out a fish dinner!

THE END

Easy, ma'am! I didn't mean to be rude.

Why don't you just sit back down . . .

Sit down? Now? I'm wide awake!

I'll sit down when I'm ready to sleep! Until then, I'm going to keep swinging until I smash you!

Raven looks up at the sun. "Maybe I can trick this old giant into thinking it's nighttime," she thinks. She flies as high as she can and moves in small circles. The fog hat spills out more mist. Soon a black shadow falls across the giant.

"Where did the sun go?" calls the giant.

"It's gone!" yells Raven. "Night is here!"

The old giant lets her arms drop to her sides and yawns. "Good!" she growls. "I don't have the energy for long days like this anymore." She plops back down on the beach with a CRASH.

"I'm going to take this hat back to that goat!" thinks Raven. "I'm too worn out for more tricks!"

THE END

"If I change into a fish, that pelican might try to hook me," thinks Raven. "Then I can change back and fly away with his pole!" With a flash of light, she becomes a fish and flops into the water.

"I might as well see if that fish will bite," says Mr. Pelican. He casts out his fishing line. Raven grabs it with her fishy lips.

"Now to change back and grab the pole," thinks Raven. Then she sees the magic box sinking into the deep. Without feet and claws, she can't hold on to it! "I can still get out of this," she thinks, as the pelican stuffs her in his basket with the other fish.

She's only kidding herself. For Raven the fish, this is

THE END

Mr. Goat, that is an AMAZING hat, if I may say so.

It's not amazing. It's a NUISANCE! I can't ever see where I'm going.

Then why don't you take it off?

My head sunburns easily. Better to bump into things than to have a roasted noggin, that's what I think!

Well, where did you get it? I could use a magic hat!

If it's magic you're wanting, talk to the beavers. They're a mean bunch, but they've got a magic painting.

Their lodge is over yonder.

A magic painting! I wonder what it does . . .

Go on to the next page.

"I could knock on the lodge door and ask to see the painting," says Raven to herself. "But the old goat said these beavers are mean. Maybe I should hide behind that log and wait for them to leave. Then I could sneak in!"

If Raven knocks on the lodge door,

TURN TO PAGE **11.**

If Raven hides behind the old log,

TURN TO PAGE **58.**

Raven holds the box and tries to think. But she can't think of anything bigger than a whale!

The huge mouth is almost around her when she thinks of a solution. She won't get bigger. She'll get so small that the killer whale won't be able to bite her! With a flash of light, Raven changes into a water bug. The whale chomps down, but the current sweeps Raven safely away.

"Good thing I'm so clever!" says Raven. "Now to change back..."

Raven looks around. She's not holding the box anymore. The whale must have swallowed it!

"Oh, no!" she says. "I'm going to be stuck as a bug forever!" It looks as if Raven's days as a bird have reached

THE END

Ha ha ha! Now THAT is a good trick!

Are you sure you know your part?

Yes, yes. Take the hat and go!

Crow! Hey, Crow!

What do you want, old goat? You're not still mad about those cabbages, I hope!

Not me! I'm here to warn you. I just saw a big thundercloud out by the beach. It told me it was on its way to see you!

"Why would a thundercloud want to visit ME?" asks Crow.

"It saw you out before the storm and fell in love with you," says the old goat. "Be careful! A thundercloud shakes you instead of hugging you. It throws lightning bolts instead of blowing kisses."

Crow jumps to his feet. "A cloud in LOVE? You're pulling my leg!"

"No, I'm not!" says the goat, pointing. "Look!"

Crow sees a huge cloud of fog coming toward his nest. He lets out a terrified caw and flies away.

Raven starts to laugh. She bursts through the fake cloud made by the goat's hat.

"That was a fine trick!" says the old goat as Raven drops the hat on his head.

And he's right!

THE END

Raven puts the box in her mouth so that she won't drop it. With a big flash, Raven suddenly looks like a fish! She starts to swim around and hears a laugh behind her. She turns and sees a mean-looking sturgeon. The big fish is twice her size!

"You look pretty tasty," says the sturgeon. Its toothy mouth is open wide.

Raven thinks hard. There's another quick flash of light. In place of the small fish is a sea lion!

"Get out of here, you!" says Raven in a growly sea lion voice. The sturgeon turns around and swims away as fast as he can.

Raven likes being big and tough! Then she hears a deep rumble behind her. A killer whale is coming her way. And its mouth is open wide!

If Raven tries to use the box to change into something bigger than the whale,

TURN TO PAGE 39.

If Raven tries to reason with the whale,

TURN TO PAGE 18.

LOTS of animals can sing. I must have PERFORMERS! Animals who can sing in front of LARGE CROWDS without getting NERVOUS!

I can do that! I can sing in front of crowds!

Then GATHER a crowd. We'll have a PARTY!

A party?

A party! Invite your friends, and fix lots of food. Do you have family in the area?

Well, my cousin Raven lives nearby.

Then treat her like the guest of honor! It's what the king would want.

Yes, sir! I'll get right on it, sir!

If I'm a bit late, don't be afraid to start without me!

Ha ha ha!

Later that night, Raven is wrapped in Crow's warmest blanket. She eats her forty-fifth cheese cracker while Crow sings. His voice is awfully scratchy, but the party guests don't seem to mind. They're all enjoying the food.

Raven sits at the head of the table. Everyone assumes that it is her party, not Crow's. "What a great party, Raven," they all say. "We must have our own parties and invite you!"

"Oh, please do!" says Raven. She hopes they'll invite Crow too. He'll need cheering up when he figures out he was tricked!

THE END

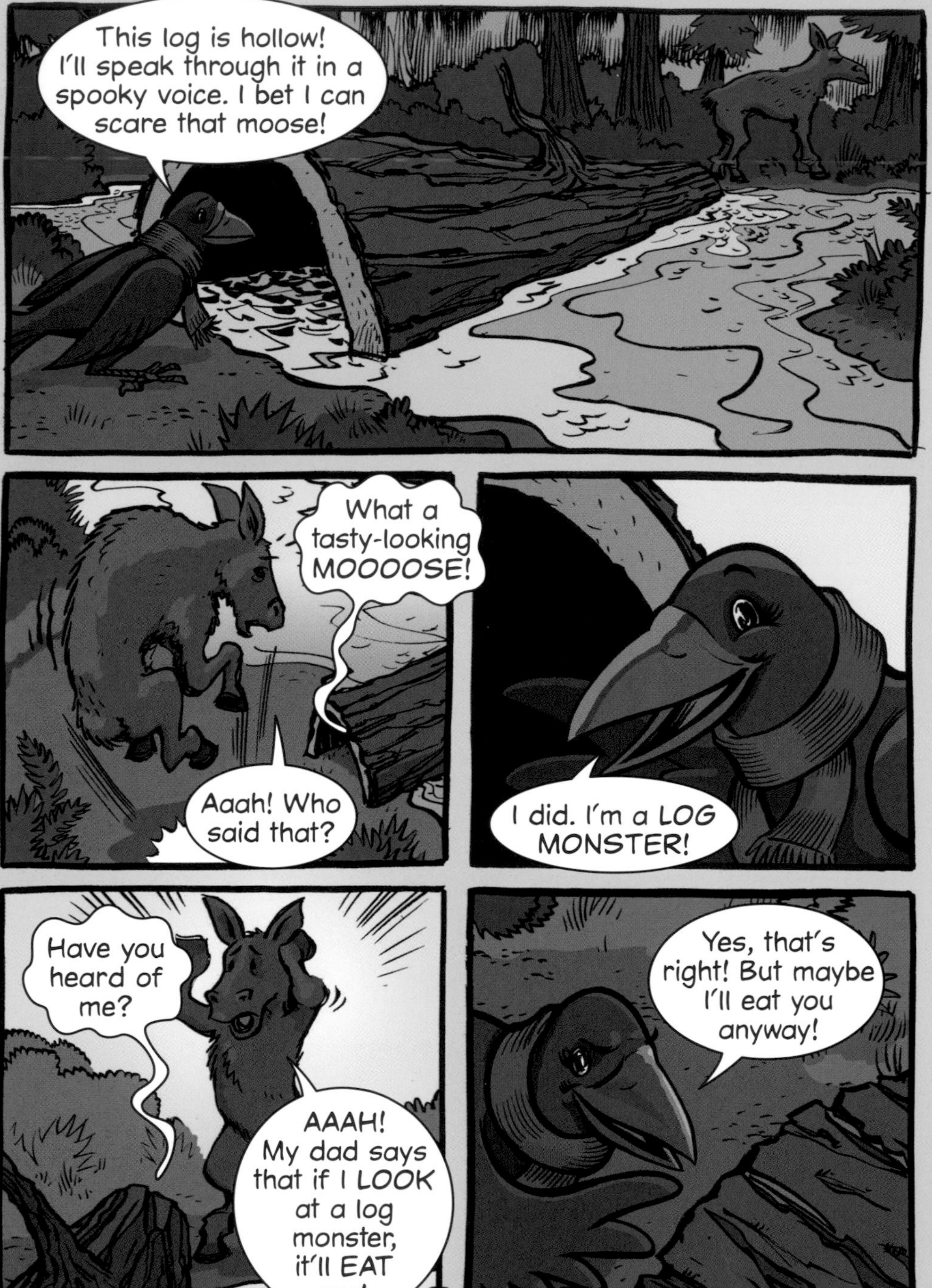
This log is hollow! I'll speak through it in a spooky voice. I bet I can scare that moose!
What a tasty-looking MOOOOSE!
Aaah! Who said that?
I did. I'm a LOG MONSTER!
Have you heard of me?
AAAH! My dad says that if I LOOK at a log monster, it'll EAT me!
Yes, that's right! But maybe I'll eat you anyway!

Go on to the next page.

"Nooo!" screams the little moose. He runs off into the woods.

Raven laughs. "I taught that naughty moose a lesson!" she thinks. Then she notices the fog swirling around her. "What's that?! Now I'M scared!" she says.

She flies above the fog. It's thickest near the beach.

"So that's where the fog is coming from!" says Raven.

Raven spots an old goat walking down the beach. The goat is wearing a wide-brimmed hat. But it's no ordinary hat. Fog is pouring out from underneath the brim. Soon fog covers the whole beach.

Go on to the next page.

"What an amazing hat!" says Raven. "I could play all kinds of tricks with a hat like that!"

If Raven asks the goat where he got the hat,

TURN TO PAGE 37.

If Raven tries to take the hat off the goat's head,

TURN TO PAGE 14.

If Raven tries to get the goat to help her play a trick,

TURN TO PAGE 20.

What should I be? A mouse? A squirrel? No, I've got it . . .
. . . a GRIZZLY BEAR!
Wow! That IS a lot warmer! No wonder bears sleep for so long--I feel like I'm wrapped up in a big, soft blanket!
Ow! Ow ow ow! Somebody help!
Ow! There's a thorn in my foot, and I can't reach it! Please, somebody help me pull it out!

Go on to the next page.

"That's Seagull!" thinks Raven. "He's always up to no good. But I should still help him if he's hurt." She starts to lumber toward him. Then remembers her new shape. "Oh my!" she thinks. "I bet I look pretty scary. Maybe I should change back into my regular body. Then again, I am SO very warm and comfortable..."

If Raven changes back into her bird body,

TURN TO PAGE
29.

If Raven decides to stay in her bear body,

TURN TO PAGE
7.

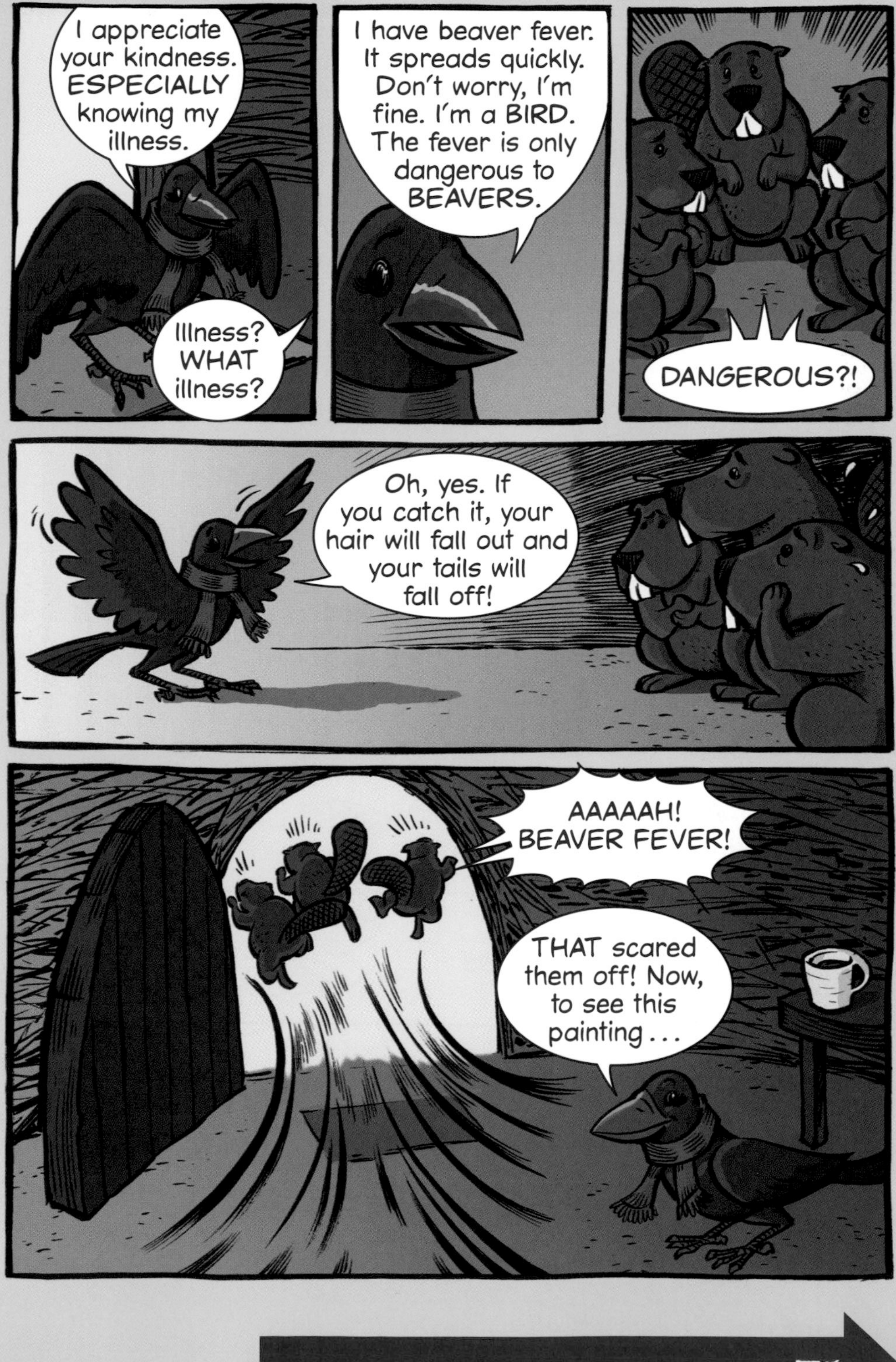
I appreciate your kindness. ESPECIALLY knowing my illness.
Illness? WHAT illness?
I have beaver fever. It spreads quickly. Don't worry, I'm fine. I'm a BIRD. The fever is only dangerous to BEAVERS.
DANGEROUS?!
Oh, yes. If you catch it, your hair will fall out and your tails will fall off!
AAAAAH! BEAVER FEVER!
THAT scared them off! Now, to see this painting . . .

Go on to the next page.

Raven looks at the picture. "That's not a painting at all!" she says. "The river's moving!"

Raven steps toward it and trips. "Oh, no!" she yells. She tumbles head over heels.

Raven expects a loud crash. Instead, she falls INTO the painting! She lands in the river with a loud splash.

"Well, well!" a booming voice says. Raven looks up to the sky. The beavers stare back down at her, as big as mountains. "We ran back in when we heard that clatter. Looks like you're stuck in our magic painting!"

Raven watches the beavers roll up the painting. The ground seems to turn upside down. Everything goes dark. Her days of freedom have reached

THE END

It's a cabin!

Come on, Mrs. Pelican, open up. It's time to catch our dinner.

All right, Mr. Pelican.

Let me just pour some water in.

How silly! The husband cast his line into the wife's beak! He won't catch any fish THAT way!

You cook the first fish. I'll take the others to market.

YOU cook the fish! I want to go to market!

Mr. Pelican gathers up nine fish and heads out the door. "You went last time. It's my turn!" he says.

Raven watches the fisherman leave. "Fish from a beak? That's a great trick!" she says to herself. "But is it the fishing pole that's special or Mrs. Pelican's beak?"

If Raven tries to trick Mrs. Pelican into letting Raven use her beak,

TURN TO PAGE 9.

If Raven changes her shape to get a hold of the fishing pole,

TURN TO PAGE 36.

"Granny Mouse," says Raven, "I have to tell you something. I'm really a raven. I have a magic box that lets me change into other animals."

"That's just wonderful, dear," says Granny Mouse.

"I'm only a bear because I was so cold," says Raven. "The storm blew away my blanket."

"Why don't you change into a sheep?" asks Granny Mouse, "I'll shear your wool and make you a new blanket!"

"Great idea!" says Raven. She grabs the magic box. With a flash, she changes into a sheep!

Granny Mouse pulls out a pair of clipping shears. "Much better!" she says. "I wondered how you were going to fit at the tea table!"

Raven smiles. Her quest to find warmth has reached

THE END

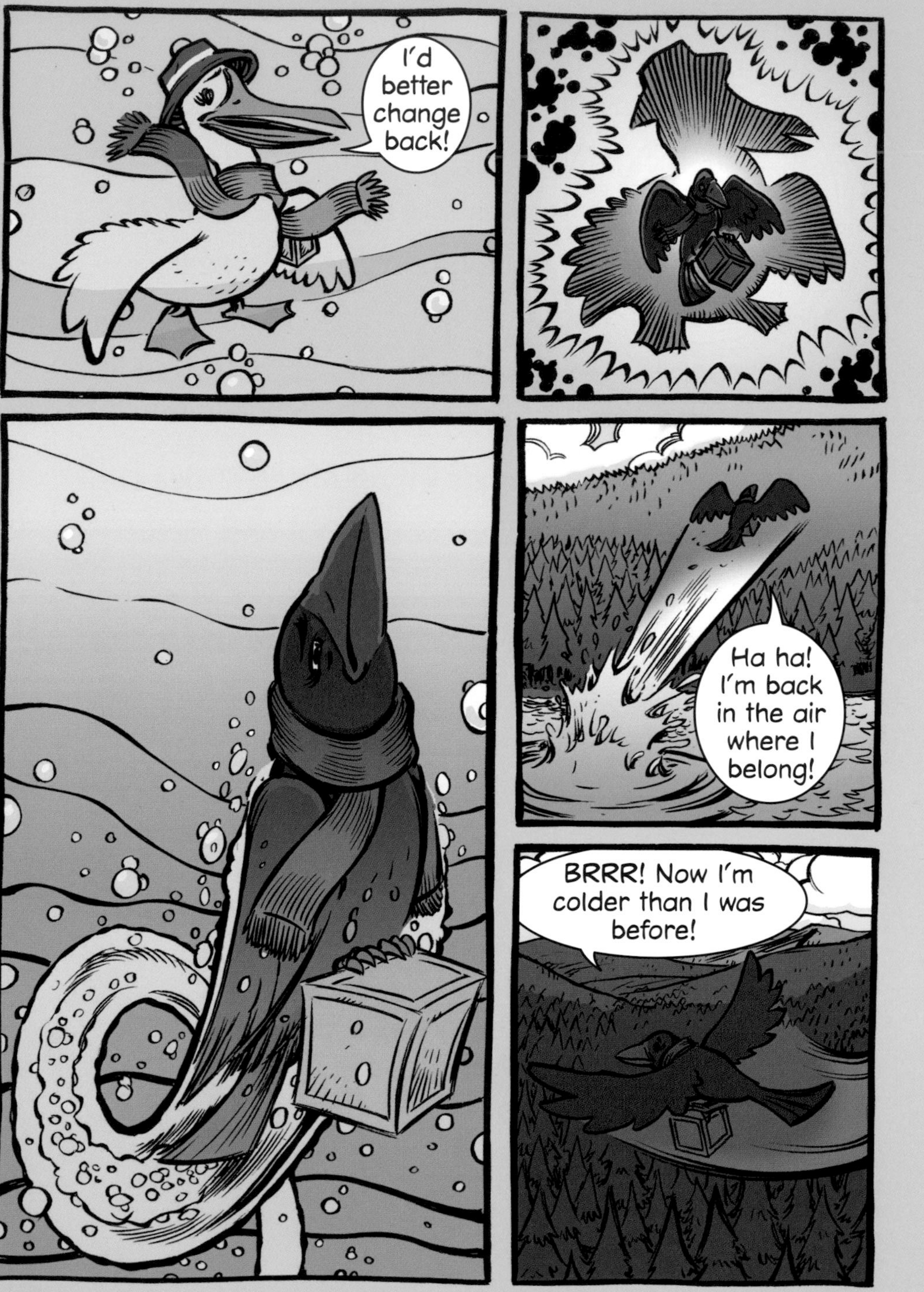
I'd better change back!
Ha ha! I'm back in the air where I belong!
BRRR! Now I'm colder than I was before!

 Go on to the next page.

Raven flies over the beach, looking for a place to land. She spots an old mouse woman pulling a cart filled with wool blankets.

"Hello, old mouse!" says Raven. "Why do you have so many blankets?"

"I take them home and unravel them," says the old mouse. "I like to roll around in shredded wool."

"May I have one?" asks Raven. "I'm very cold."

"Do you have anything to trade?" asks the old mouse.

"All I have is this magic box," Raven says. "It will let you change into anything you want."

The old mouse woman nods and hands Raven a blanket. Raven's glad to be rid of the box. It has brought her nothing but trouble!

THE END

Raven flaps down
and sits on the old log.
"Funny," she thinks.
"This log feels warm!"
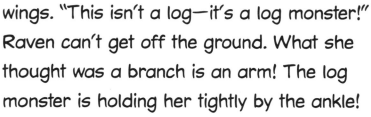
She looks at it
closely. A knot in the
wood slides open. A big
green eye looks back!

"Oh no!" Raven
thinks, flapping her
wings. "This isn't a log—it's a log monster!"
Raven can't get off the ground. What she
thought was a branch is an arm! The log
monster is holding her tightly by the ankle!

"I was hoping you'd stop to take a look,"
grumbles the monster. "I love a good bird
supper!"

Raven gulps. Maybe she can trick the log
monster into letting her go. But most likely,
this is

THE END

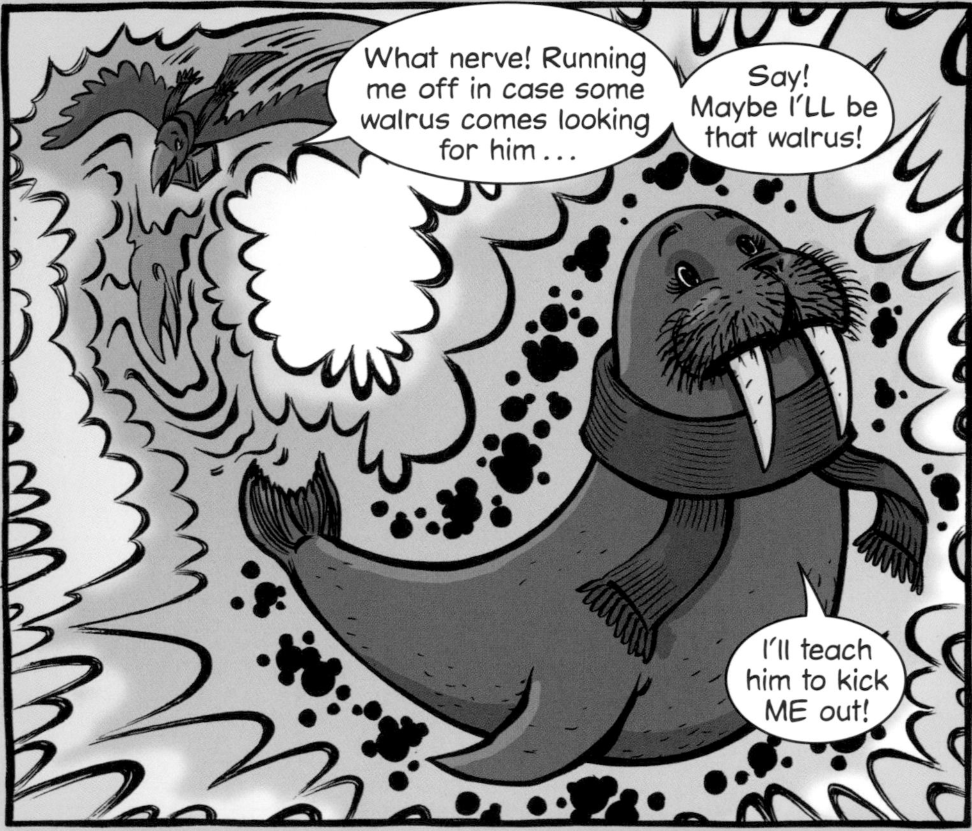
What nerve! Running me off in case some walrus comes looking for him . . .
Say! Maybe I'LL be that walrus!
I'll teach him to kick ME out!

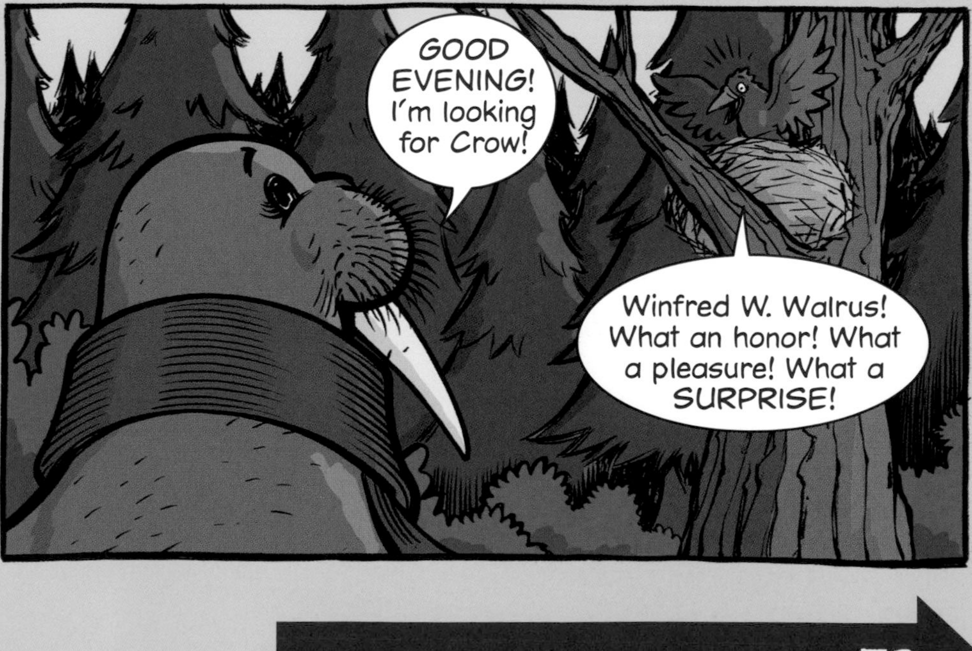
GOOD EVENING! I'm looking for Crow!
Winfred W. Walrus! What an honor! What a pleasure! What a SURPRISE!

Go on to the next page.

"Are you here to listen to me sing, Mr. Walrus?" asks Crow. "I'm VERY good. Shall I start?"

If Raven tricks Crow into leaving his nest and flying away,

TURN TO PAGE 17.

If Raven tricks Crow into throwing a party for her,

TURN TO PAGE 44.

Raven swoops around the giant's head. She leaves a thick trail of fog behind her. Soon a cloud surrounds the giant.

"Now she can't see! I can take my time," thinks Raven. She sets the hat on top of the old giant's head.

Raven flies down to the mud and starts picking up shells. "Ooh! This one's shiny," she says, wrapping it in her scarf. Suddenly a crash makes the ground shake.

Raven looks up. The giant has sat back down in the shallow water. But now the water isn't shallow anymore. It's rising in a great wave— and it's headed toward Raven!

Raven tries to fly up, but her feet are stuck in the mud. She tugs at her ankles, but the wave washes over her head. Raven is soaked again!

THE END

What're you doing?

What did you say?

PTEW!

I ASKED YOU what you're doing!

I'm looking for a spare fishing pole.

You don't OWN a spare pole. Come to think of it, you don't own a SCARF!

Um...I can explain...

Gasp! You're an impostor! HELP! HELP!

SHH! Stop yelling!

Mrs. Pelican are you all ri-- HEY! Who are YOU?

Get him, husband!

Raven tries to run, but Mrs. Pelican holds on tightly to her scarf. Mr. Pelican takes his fishing pole and whacks the impostor Mr. Pelican over the head.

"Ouch!" says Raven. "Really, I can explain!" But the Pelicans aren't likely to let up soon.

Raven breaks free and runs off into the cold woods. Mr. Pelican chases after her, still whacking at her with the fishing pole. It looks as if Raven will be pretty sore by the time this chase reaches

THE END

People across the Pacific Northwest in North America told many of the first **RAVEN** tales. The Pacific Northwest includes the states of Oregon, Washington, and Idaho, along with parts of Canada. Native Americans from the Pacific Northwest created most of the stories in this book.

The story of Raven and the fog hat comes from the Tlingit people. The story of the thorn in Seagull's foot comes from the Nootka people. The story of Raven tricking Crow into throwing her a party comes from the Salish people. A lot of the other stories come from the Haida people, such as the tale of the beavers' magic picture.

Some of the stories are the same no matter which tribe tells them. Raven can always change her shape. Granny Mouse is always looking for wool. But sometimes Raven is a boy instead of a girl! In all the tales, one thing is always true. Raven loves to play tricks!